D0536755

Waiting for Mama

Gianna Marino

Even though I can't see,
I know what's happening outside.

I can feel it,
like I can feel
the cold.

My mama's goodbye call
floats inside my shell.

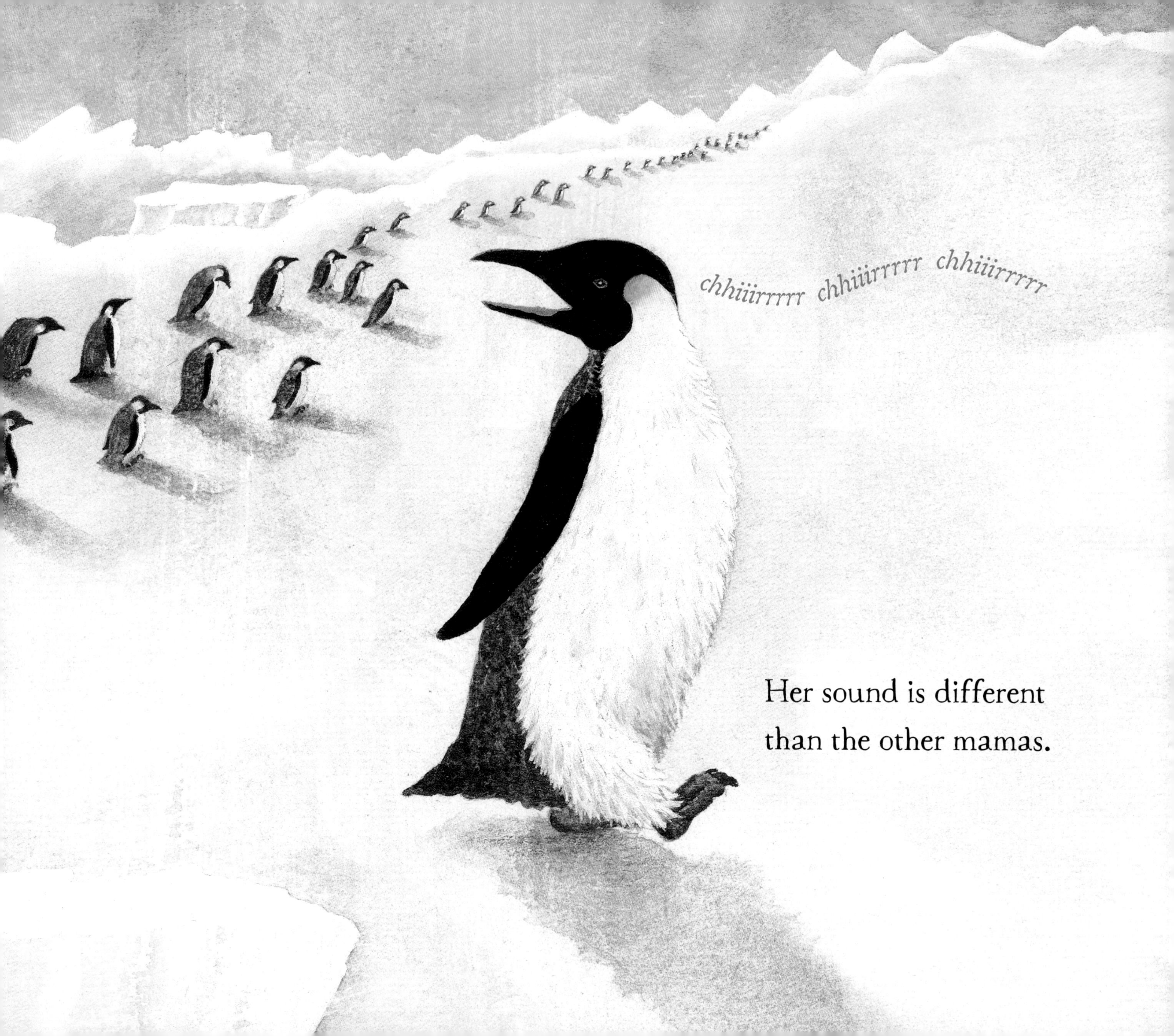

chhiiirrrrr chhiiirrrrr chhiiirrrrr

Her sound is different
than the other mamas.

Mama has to walk a long
way to find food.

The ice makes a *CRUNCH*
as the last of the mamas go.

My papa knows how to balance me
on his feet under his warm belly.

His nails *CLICK* and *CLACK* on my shell.

I hear *PEEPS* and *SQUEAKS* from
the eggs on the feet of other papas.

We are all waiting for our
mamas to come home.

Papa misses Mama.
Just like I do.

When the wind blows
hard outside,

SWWWWOOOOOOSSSSHHH

Papa goes into the huddle.
Sometimes I slip off his toes!

But Papa knows how
to roll me back under
his warm belly.

When everyone is sleeping,
all I can hear is Papa's heart.

BOOM!
BOOM!
BOOM!

My papa loves me.

I want to SEE Papa.
I want to STRETCH
my legs!

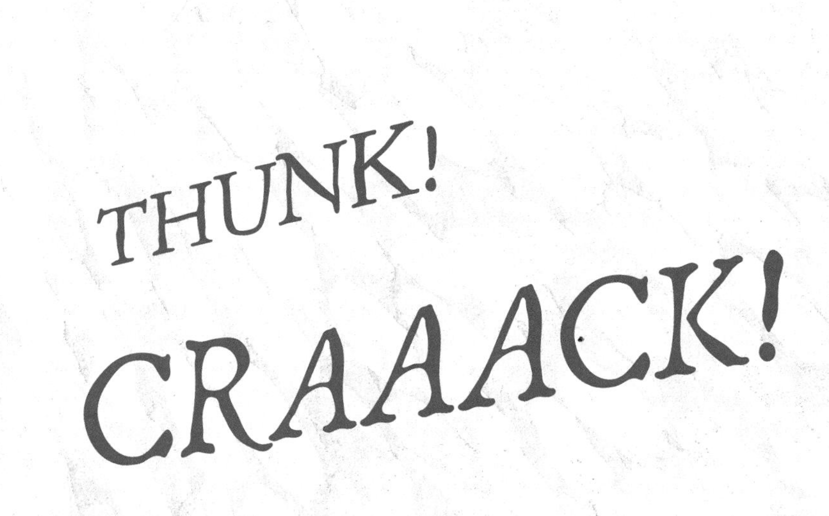
THUNK!
CRAAACK!

PEEP PEEEEEP
PEEEEEEEEEEEEEP

beep
beep

Papa! You are so big!

Are those the mamas?

honk honk honk

gaker gaker gaker

squawk sqawk squawk
cheep
cheeeep

I don't hear MY mama.

Is she coming?

chhiiirrrrr chhiiirrrrr chhiiirrrrr
Mama!

chhiiiirrrrr chhiiirrrrr chhiiirrrrr

Papa!

I can hear her heart.

BOOM!

BOOM!

BOOM!

Mama loves me, too.

A Note on Emperor Penguins

EMPEROR PENGUINS spend their entire lives on the ice or in the surrounding waters of Antartica. During the coldest, darkest time of the year, a female emperor penguin will lay a single egg, then leave to find food. She will sometimes travel over fifty miles to feed on fish, squid, and krill. The male penguin cares for the egg, balancing it on his feet and keeping it warm under his broad pouch. If the egg touches the ground, it will freeze within minutes.

To survive the harsh winds, blizzards, and temperatures as low as -76°F, male penguins huddle together, taking turns in the warm interior. The male penguins don't eat while the females are away.

After two months of feeding, the female penguin returns to feed her newly hatched chick. Her timely return is critical to the survival of the chick. Emperor penguins have special calls to find one another after their long separation.

Once the mother is back, the male can finally travel to open water to find food as well. It will be at least three years before the chick has grown enough to have a family of its own.

For my mama and papa

Thank you
for keeping me safe and warm
when I was small

VIKING
An imprint of Penguin Random House LLC, New York

First published in the United States of America by Viking, an imprint of Penguin Random House LLC, 2022

Visit us online at penguinrandomhouse.com.

Library of Congress Cataloging-in-Publication Data is available.

Manufactured in China

ISBN 9780425290705

1 3 5 7 9 10 8 6 4 2

RRD

Design by Jim Hoover   Text set in Macarons